THIS BOOK
BELONGS TO:

ISBN 978-1-5272-6623-0

Pink Robin Press
www.pinkrobinpress.co.uk

DEDICATION

This book is dedicated to my precious daughters, Sion, Joell and Ellisha Boateng. Your beauty shines both inside and out. Love always mummy.

-C.B.

To my darling daughter Janelle, mummy loves you very much. Always remember you are beautiful.

-Y.O.T.

Perfectly
Perfect Me!

Written by:
**Chantel Boateng
& Yasmin Owusu-Tutu**

Illustrated by:
**Emiliya
Bogdanova**

On a hot summer's day,
in the month of May,
Grandma wondered,
why Jenny was home today.

"Why are you not skipping,
hopping and **bopping**
all around? Why aren't
you playing with your friends,
all over town?"

"I want long straight hair like my good friend Claire, **swishing** and **swaying** it in the air".

"But your hair
is full of coils,
as bountiful as can be,
oh why, oh why don't
you see the beauty
that I see?"

"I want blue eyes like my little friend Sue, **gleaming** and **beaming,** that's all I want too."

"Your eyes are as
dark as night, but yet
they shine so bright,
with their enchanting sheen,
they're the prettiest
things I've ever seen."

"I want light skin,
like my best friend
Robin, so nice
and fair, what else
can compare?"

"Your skin is divine,
oh just look how it glistens,
soft as silk, smooth
as butter, my darling
child; I pray that you listen.
Skin like chocolate;
it's so royal and supreme, just
like our amazing
past African queens.

Even though you look **different** to your good friend Claire, swishing and swaying her long straight hair.

Even though you look different to your little friend Sue, eyes **gleaming** and beaming the colour of blue.

Even though you look
different to your best friend Robin,
with skin **so fair**, you think
nothing would compare.

There's just one thing that I want
you to know, which will surely
wash away your **sorrow**.

You are loved, appreciated,
valued and **cared for,**
Your beauty is unique
and cannot be compared.

. . .

The important lesson,
I hope you learn today,
Is that we are all
beautiful; in our own
special way."

"Oh wow! Grandma,
why didn't I see?
How **beautiful**
and **precious** my
brown skin makes me."

So, on a **hot** summer's day, in the month of May, Jenny decided she would not stay home that day.

"I'm **happy** Grandma; I no longer have a frown, I love my hair full of coils; for it is my royal crown.

I **love** my dark eyes, and chocolate coloured skin, And even if I could; I wouldn't change a thing.

So, I'm off to skipping,
hopping and
bopping all around,
playing with my friends,
all over town."